Ladybird Readers

On the Farm

Series Editor: Sorrel Pitts
Text adapted by Sorrel Pitts
Illustrated by Dan Green

LADYBIRD BOOKS

UK | USA | Canada | Ireland | Australia
India | New Zealand | South Africa

Ladybird Books is part of the Penguin Random House group of companies
whose addresses can be found at global.penguinrandomhouse.com.
www.penguin.co.uk   www.puffin.co.uk   www.ladybird.com

Penguin
Random House
UK

First published 2016
003

Copyright © Ladybird Books Ltd, 2016

The moral rights of the author and illustrator have been asserted.

Printed in China

A CIP catalogue record for this book is available from the British Library

ISBN: 978-0-241-25413-4

On the Farm

Contents

Picture words 6

Farms are for you 8

Cows live on the farm 10

Sheep live on the farm 12

Hens give us eggs 14

Baby animals 16

Food on the farm 18

Food from wheat 20

Machines on the farm 22

More machines! 24

Come to the farm 26

Activities 28

Picture words

 calf

 farmer

 hen

 lamb

 machine

tractor

vegetable

wheat

wool

Farms are for you

Our food comes from farms. Farmers have got animals, too.

Sheep give us their wool.

The farmer drives his tractor.

Our milk comes from cows.

Cows live on the farm

There are cows on the farm and we get milk from them.

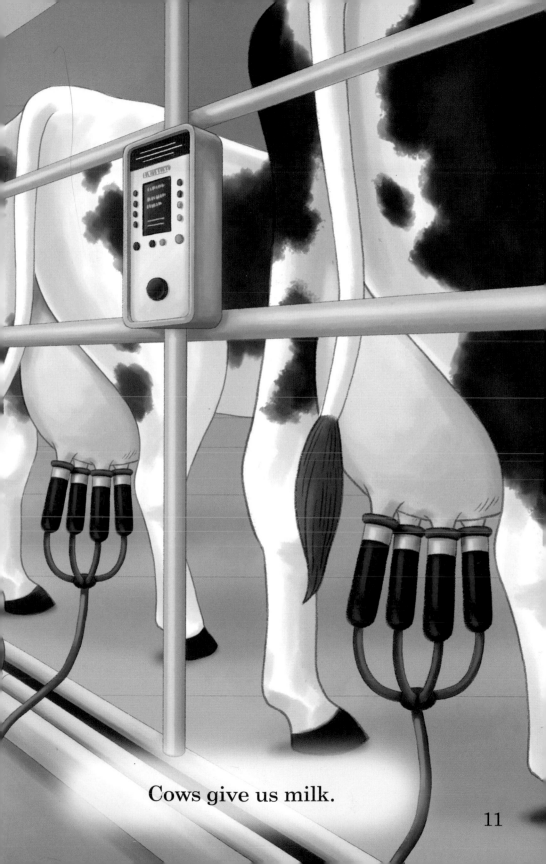

Cows give us milk.

Sheep live on the farm

Our wool comes from sheep.

The sheepdog helps the farmer with her sheep.

farmer

sheepdog

The sheepdog runs
behind the sheep.

Hens give us eggs

There are many hens on the farm. These hens give us eggs.

hens

The farmer's hens give him lots of eggs. 15

Baby animals

This girl helps the
new lambs.

lambs

Lambs are baby sheep.

This boy helps the new calves, too.

calves

Calves are baby cows.

Food on the farm

Many farmers have got wheat on their farms.

This farmer has got vegetables on his farm, too.

wheat

vegetables

In September, the farmer puts the
vegetables and wheat in boxes.

Food from wheat

There is wheat in lots
of our food.

wheat

We make bread and cakes with wheat.

Machines on the farm

Machines help farmers.
This farmer has got
a tractor.

tractor

The farmer puts the food
behind her tractor.

23

More machines!

Machines help farmers with their wheat and vegetables.

Machines can do many jobs on the farm.

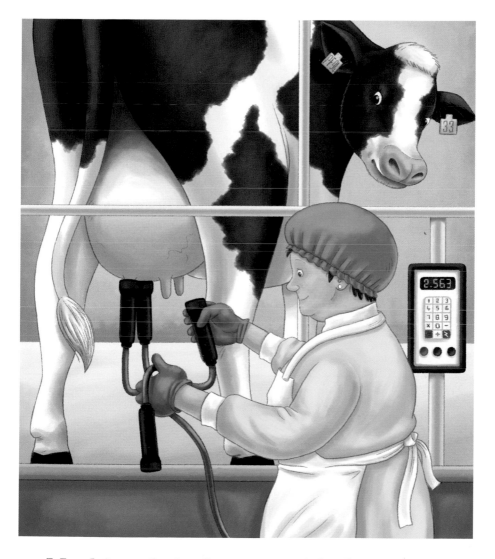

Machines help farmers with their cows.

Come to the farm

You can go to some farms and see their lambs and calves.

Lambs and calves are very small!

You can see the machines, too.

Activities

The key below describes the skills practiced in each activity.

📝 Spelling and writing

📖 Reading

💬 Speaking

❓ Critical thinking

✴ Preparation for the Cambridge Young Learners Exams

Look and read.
Put a ✓ **or a** ✗ **in the box.**  ⬤ ⬤

1  These animals are sheep.

2  This is a sheepdog.

3  This is a tractor.

4  This is a farmer.

5  This is a lamb.

2 Look and read. Write yes or no.

Cows live on the farm

There are cows on the farm and we get milk from them.

Cows give us milk.

10   11

1 The cows are running.   no

2 We get milk from wheat.   ....

3 Machines help farmers.   ....

4 There are two cows.   ....

5 There are two farmers.   ....

3 **Circle the correct sentence.**

1  **a** Our food comes from farms.
b Our clothes come from farms.

2  **a** Farmers have got animals.
b Farmers have not got sheepdogs.

3  **a** The girl gives milk to a sheep.
b The girl gives milk to a lamb.

4  **a** Hens give us wool.
b Hens give us eggs.

4 **Ask and answer *How many?* questions with a friend.**

Example:

How many lambs are there?

There are four lambs.

5 Circle the correct word.

Sheep live on the farm
Our wool comes from sheep.
The sheepdog helps the farmer with her sheep.

farmer

sheepdog

The sheepdog runs behind the sheep.

12

13

1 The sheepdog helps the farmer with her **cows** / **sheep**.

2 Our wool comes from **sheepdogs** / **sheep**.

3 This sheepdog is running **in front of** / **behind** the sheep.

4 The farmer is wearing a green **jacket** / **hat**.

5 The farmer is a **man** / **woman**.

6 Look and read.
Write yes or no. 📖 ✏️ ⬡

Food on the farm

Many farmers have got wheat on their farms.

This farmer has got vegetables on his farm, too.

wheat

vegetables

In September, the farmer puts the vegetables and wheat in boxes.

19

1 Food comes from farms.   _yes_

2 Many farmers have not got wheat on their farms.   ....

3 Some farmers have got vegetables on their farms.   ....

4 The farmer puts vegetables in boxes in April.   ....

5 The woman has got vegetables in her hands.   ....

7 **Ask and answer questions about the pictures with a friend.** ●

The farmer drives his tractor.

Our milk comes from cows.

9

Food from wheat

There is wheat in lots of our food.

wheat

Example:

Are there cows on the farm?

Yes, there are.

8 Write the missing letters.

act   am   eat   he   abl

1  w h e a t

2  v e g e t _____ e s

3  t r _____ o r

4  s _____ e p

5  l _____ b

9 Look and read.
Circle the correct pictures.

1 This comes from wheat.

 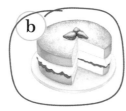 

2 These come from hens.

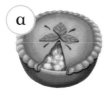  

3 This comes from sheep.

4 This comes from cows.

 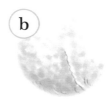 

10 **Match the two parts of the sentence.**

Machines can do many jobs on the farm.

Machines help farmers with their cows.

25

Come to the farm
You can go to some farms and see their lambs and calves.

Lambs and calves are very small!

26

1 Machines can

2 Machines help farmers with

3 You can

4 You can see little

5 You can see big

a go to some farms.

b do many jobs on the farm.

c cows and sheep.

d calves and lambs.

e their cows.

38

11 Ask and answer *Do you?* and *Have you got?* questions with a friend. ◖

Example:

Do you eat wheat?

Yes, I eat wheat.

. . . a favorite animal?

. . . eat eggs?

. . . animals at home?

12 Look and read.
Put a ✓ or a X in the box. 📖 ✿

Food from wheat

There is wheat in lots
of our food.

wheat

1 Can you see a cat? ✓

2 Can you see a farmer?

3 Can you see a lot of eggs?

4 Can you see five bags of wheat?

5 Can you see the trees?

13 **Write the questions.** 📖 ✏️

1 (is) (Where) (the) (farmer) (?)

   Where is the farmer?

2 (this) (his) (Is) (cow) (?)

3 (Are) (brown) (these) (eggs) (?)

4 (milk) (Do) (you) (like) (?)

5 (lambs) (Can) (the) (see) (you) (?)

14 **Ask and answer the questions with a friend.**

1

> *Where do eggs come from?*

> *Eggs come from hens.*

2 Where does milk come from?

3 Where do our vegetables come from?

4 Do you eat wheat for breakfast and lunch?

5 Do you eat vegetables with your dinner?

15 Look and read.
Circle *yes* or *no*.

This boy helps the new calves, too.

calves

Calves are baby cows.

17

Machines on the farm

Machines help farmers. This farmer has got a tractor.

tractor

22

1 Farmers like animals. (**yes**) **no**

2 Farmers like working with machines. **yes** **no**

3 Farmers work in the house. **yes** **no**

4 Farmers wear beautiful clothes. **yes** **no**

5 Farmers drive tractors. **yes** **no**

16 Look again at the pictures in 15. Talk to your teacher. 🗨

1

> What are the calves doing?

> They are sleeping.

2 What is the mother cow doing?

3 Do you like calves and lambs?

4 What is the woman farmer doing?

5 Would you like to do her job?

17 **Look and read.**
Put a ☑ or a ☒ in the box. 📖 ✿

1 These foods come from wheat. ✓

2 There are vegetables in a cake. ☐

3 There is wheat in this. ☐

4 There is wheat in this. ☐

5  There is wheat in vegetables. ☐

18 Look at the pictures. Look at the letters. Write the words.

1    g e s g

e g g s

2    m e r f a r

3    e a t w h

4    o l o w

5    g e v e b l e s t a

19 Find the words.

tractor

machine

wheat

farmer

hens

calves

tjblf (tractor) bercofghensgelymachinecalveswheatcabrssfarmerlerhle

Level 1

Anansi Helps a Friend

978–0–241–25409–7

Cinderella

978–0–241–25407–3

The Enormous Turnip

978–0–241–25408–0

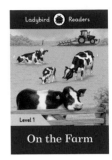

On the Farm

978–0–241–25413–4

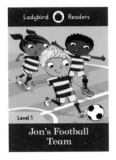

Jon's Football Team

978–0–241–25411–0

The Magic Porridge Pot

978–0–241–25406–6

In the Garden

978–0–241–26220–7

Fun with Old Things

978–0–241–26219–1

Peter Rabbit Goes to the Island

978–0–241–25415–8

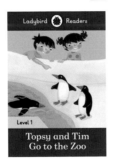

Topsy and Tim Go to the Zoo

978–0–241–25414–1

Now you're ready for Level 2!

Notes
CEFR levels are based on guidelines set out in the Council of Europe's European Framework. Cambridge Young Learners English (YLE) Exams give a reliable indication of a child's progression in learning English.